A GARDENER'S ALPHABET

BY MARY AZARIAN

HOUGHTON MIFFLIN COMPANY
BOSTON

The illustrations are woodcuts, hand tinted with watercolors.

Library of Congress Cataloging-in-Publication Data

Azarian, Mary.
A gardener's alphabet / by Mary Azarian.
p. cm.
Summary: An alphabet book featuring words associated with gardening, including
bulbs, compost, digging, insects, and weeds.
RNF ISBN 0-618-03380-7   PAP ISBN 0-618-54881-5
1. Gardening — Juvenile literature. 2. Gardens — Juvenile literature.
3. English language — Alphabet — Juvenile literature. [1. Gardening. 2. Alphabet.]
I. Title.
SB457.A92 2000
635 — dc21
[[E]]
99-044242

PAP ISBN-13: 978-0618-54881-1

Printed in China
SCP   13 12 11 10
4500404683

For Grandma Annie and Uncle Winnie,
who taught me to love gardens,
and with thanks to Elizabeth for "H"
to Janet for "L"
to Terry for "N"
and to Joyce for "U"

Mary and her grandmother, Annie

GARDENS HAVE ALWAYS PLAYED AN IMPORTANT PART IN MY LIFE. AMONG MY EARLIEST memories was the large garden in my grandmother's back yard. The tiny, delicate blue and white violets scattered across the lawn in early spring were a wonder to me. In summer red roses nearly obscured the garage, and there seemed to be an endless supply of fresh vegetables. A few years later we moved to the small farm where my uncle raised a market garden of fruits, vegetables, and flowers. Tomatoes never tasted as good as they did eaten right in the field, sun-warmed and full of juice and flavor.

And so it seemed natural for me to start a garden when, as a young adult, I moved to a small hill farm in Vermont. I envisioned a lovely country cottage garden, roses and holly-hocks around the door, an effortless profusion of flowers, and an abundance of fresh vegetables for the table. The first year saw a garden full of weeds and pathetically puny vegetables. The flowers fared no better. It was not as easy as it had looked. I suppose it was then that I began the long journey to becoming a true gardener.

After almost forty years of growing all manner of plants, I have almost learned how to garden. I am convinced that gardening is the most difficult of the arts. Not only must the gardener master the elements of design and color, she must also study and learn the features and requirements of plants and come to understand the idiosyncrasies of her particular piece of land and the climate in which she gardens. As if that weren't enough, the ficklenesses of weather—the hailstorm that shreds the irises, the wind that takes down ancient trees, the drought that shrivels the corn, the frost that wipes out the tomatoes—are a constant source of frustration. Neglect the garden for a season and it all but disappears in a sea of weeds. At times it seems just too difficult. And, of course, it can be devilishly expensive. Better to abandon the whole garden and take an extended trip.

But, the garden provides such an intriguing challenge and is such a source of wonder and joy that not to garden is unthinkable. Every year features many unexpected delights—self-sown plant combinations that, in addition to being incredibly beautiful, are humbling, as they are usually far more successful than the gardener's most carefully planned efforts. The morning walk through the garden to see what has emerged from the soil or come into bloom is a perfect start to the day. And even weeding, which many people (usually nongardeners) consider a tedious chore, can be an immensely absorbing and satisfying way to spend an afternoon. Those of us fortunate enough to live in the north have the winter in which to recover and dream about next year's garden. I know that as long as I can clutch a trowel I will be a gardener. In the words of a Chinese proverb, "If you would be happy for life, plant a garden."

—MARY AZARIAN

ARBOR

COMPOST

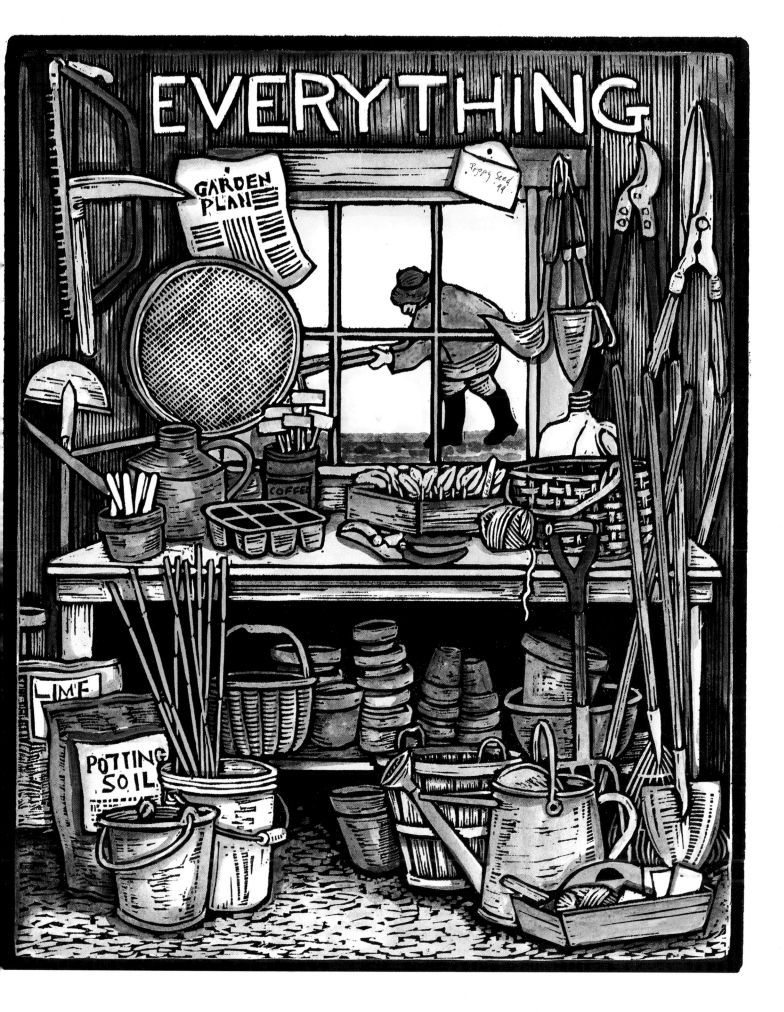

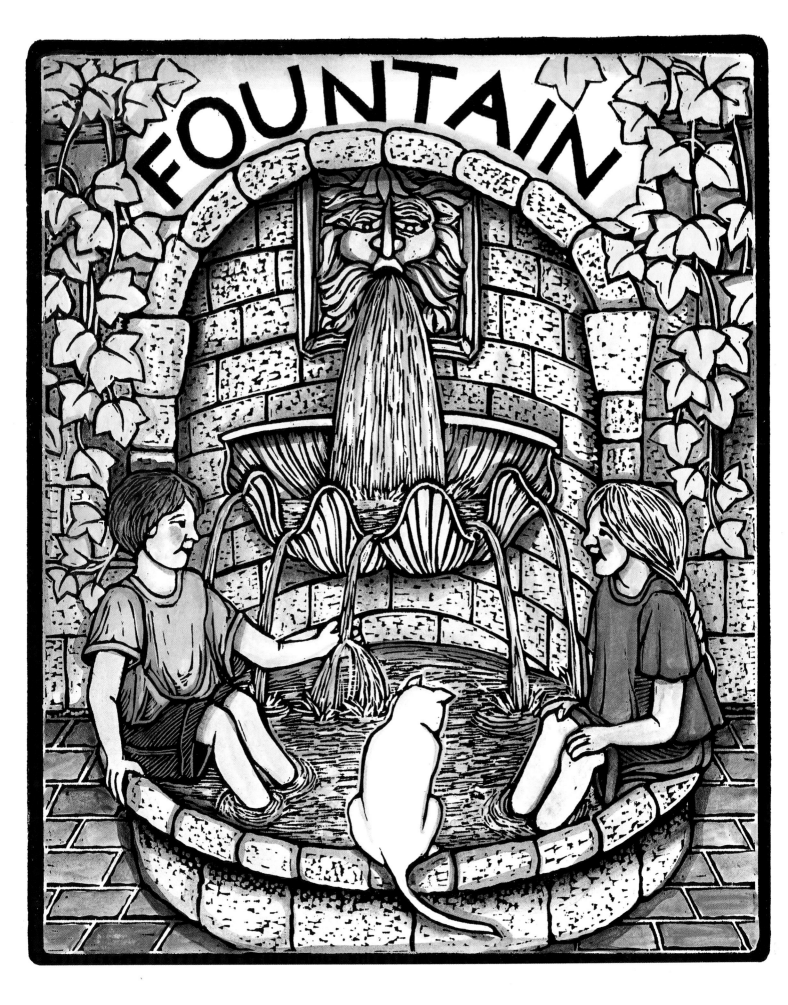

GREENHOUSE

HARVEST

INSECTS

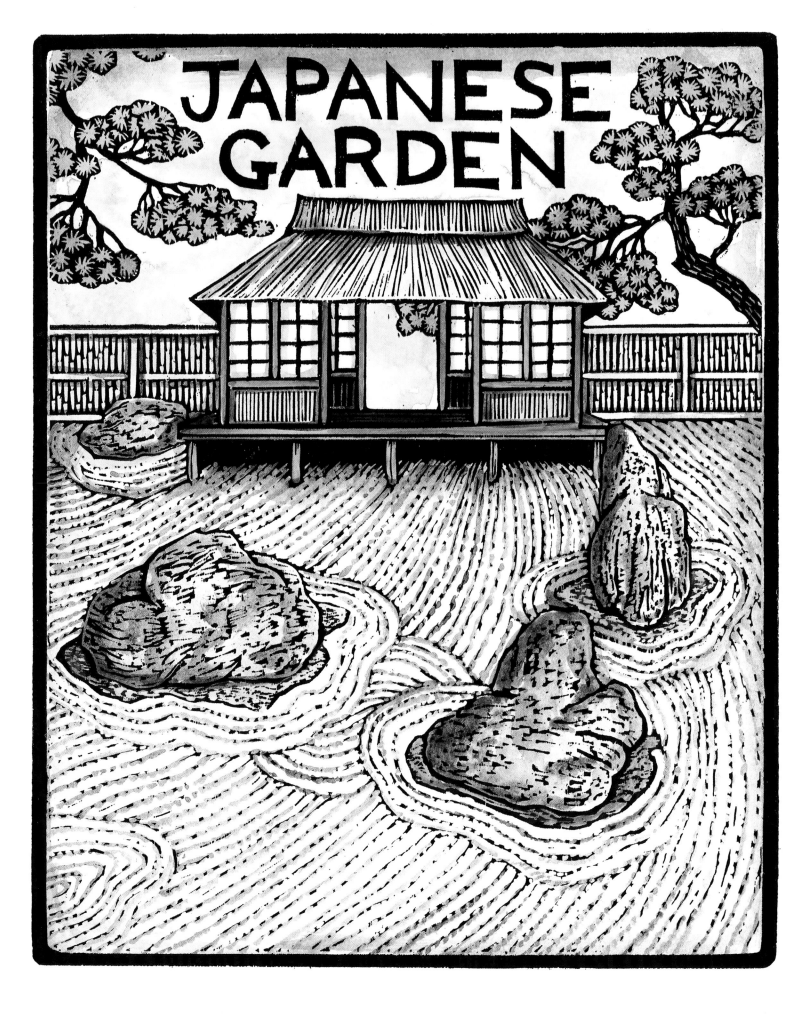

LAWN
ORNAMENTS

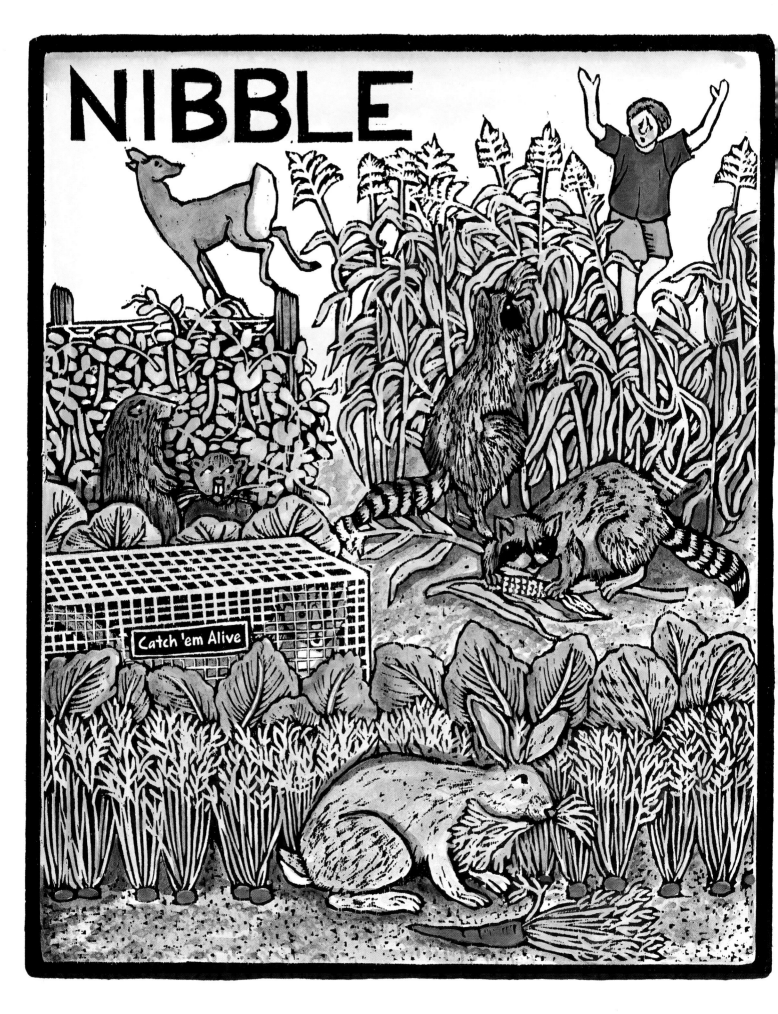

ORNAMENTAL GRASSES

QUEEN ANNE'S LACE

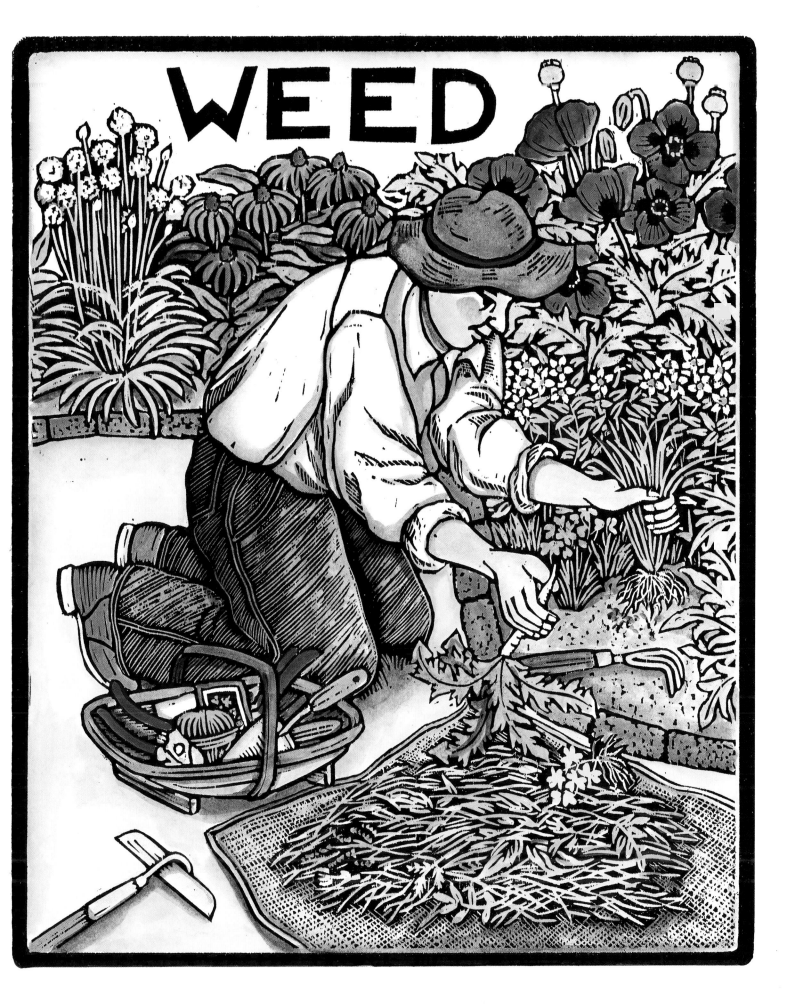

XERISCAPE

YARD